오늘의 운세

도서출판 아시아에서는 《바이링궐 에디션 한국 대표 소설》을 기획하여 한국의 우수한 문학을 주제별로 엄선해 국내외 독자들에게 소개합니다. 이 기획은 국내외 우수한 번역가들이 참여하여 원작의 품격을 최대한 살렸습니다. 문학을 통해 아시아의 정체성과 가치를 살피는 데 주력해 온 도서출판 아시아는 한국인의 삶을 넓고 깊게 이해하는 데 이 기획이 기여하기를 기대합니다.

Asia Publishers presents some of the very best modern Korean literature to readers worldwide through its new Korean literature series 〈Bilingual Edition Modern Korean Literature〉. We are proud and happy to offer it in the most authoritative translation by renowned translators of Korean literature. We hope that this series helps to build solid bridges between citizens of the world and Koreans through a rich in-depth understanding of Korea.

바이링궐 에디션 한국 대표 소설 056

Bi-lingual Edition Modern Korean Literature 056

Today's Fortune

한창훈
오늘의 운세

Han Chang-hoon

ASIA
PUBLISHERS

Contents

오늘의 운세

Today's Fortune

동네는 조용하다. 응달 처마에 낱개로 매달린 고드름 끝에서 햇살이 차갑게 반사되고 있다. 컹컹컹. 어디에 선가 개 짖는 소리가 낮게 가라앉은 공기를 깨워보기도 하지만 이내 조용해진다. 멀리 식장산 나무들은 무성한 잎 다 떨구고 가녀린 몸이 되어 차가운 공기에 조용히 떨고 있다. 저 깊은 산 어느 돌 밑에서 시작해 수원지까지 흘러내려오는 냇물도 얼굴이 꽁꽁 얼어 하얗게 비늘을 만들어내고 있을 것이다.

몸뻬 차림의 퍼머머리 여자가 종종걸음으로 스쳐 가는데 펑퍼짐한 엉덩이 굴곡을 따라 속고쟁이 선이 뚜렷하게 드러난다. 지남철처럼 쫓아가 달라붙는 시선을 애

The neighbourhood was still. Sunlight glinted off the tips of the icicles hanging from the eaves. The muffled bark of a dog cut the still air, which was immediately reclaimed by silence. The trees on Shikjang Mountain in the distance were shedding their thick foliage, trembling noiselessly as they grew slender. The surface of a brook, which trickled out from beneath some rock deep in the mountain down to a reservoir, was hardening into frozen white scales.

A woman with permed hair hurried past in baggy pants, the line of her bloomers tracing the curve of her well-rounded bottom. With great difficulty,

써 거두며 용표는 기어를 변속한다. 아무쪼록 눈조심, 입조심, 손조심. 그는 집 나설 때 아로새겼던 다짐을 다시 한 번 떠올렸다.

차는 마을 앞 자그마한 공터에 섰다. 조무래기 서넛이 햇살 바른 곳에서 땅바닥에 코를 박고 무언가를 만지고 있다가 고개를 든다. 낯바닥들이 추위에 벌겋게 달아 있다. 용표는 씨익 웃음을 흘렸으나 아이들은 소매로 코를 한 번씩 닦고는 다시 고개를 처박는데 보아하니 연 날릴 채비를 하는 모양이다.

확성기를 튼다.

"계란이 왔어요, 계란. 굵고 싱싱한 계란이 스무 개에 천팔백 원. 사십 개에 삼천사백 원. 태화농장에서 위생적으로 생산한 값싸고 싱싱한 계란이 왔어요."

가시가 앙상한 탱자나무 울타리에서 참새들이 포르르 날아오른다.

"아. 시끄러."

공터 한쪽을 지키고 있는 세천상회의 노랑 테이프 대각선 땜질 문이 드르륵 열리고 아줌마가 나타났다.

"안녕허유?"

"아이구, 그눔의 마이크 소리 땜에 안녕 못햐."

Yong-pyo tore his magnet-like gaze away from her and sped up. *Watch your eyes, mouth, and hands—* the resolution he had made when he left the house.

He pulled his truck to a stop in the small vacant lot in front of the village. In a patch of sunlight a group of children were huddled around something on the ground. They were touching it, their noses practically buried in whatever it was, and then raising their heads to look around. Their faces were flushed a ruddy red from the cold. Yong-pyo grinned. The kids gave their noses a swipe with their sleeves before lowering their heads once more. It looked like they were preparing to fly a kite.

"Eggs, eggs, get your eggs! Big fresh eggs, twenty for 1,800 *won*, thirty for 3,400 *won*! Cheap and fresh, produced hygienically on Taehwa Farms!" blared a loudspeaker from Yong-pyo's truck.

Sparrows took to the air with a flutter from the hedge of thorny orange trees.

"Bah, be quiet." The door of the Secheon Corner restaurant, slashed diagonally by yellow tape, rattled open. A woman appeared from the building, which stood on one side of the empty lot.

"헤헷, 장사는 워떠유?"

"해동도 안 됐는디 장사는 무슨, 아이구 왜 이리 춥디야."

"겨울에도 심심찮게 놀러 오던디."

이곳 세천동에는 공원이 있어 날 풀린 봄부터 가을 단풍철까지 사람이 들끓는 곳인데 요즘같이 추운 겨울에도 자가용들이 들락거리고 심각한 얼굴의 청춘남녀 발길도 끊이지 않는다.

공원 입구의 번듯한 음식점들 때문에 한 뼘쯤 내려앉아 보이는 세천상회는 요즘 것에 밀려난 고랫것으로 보인다. 그러나 그게 아니다.

세천상회에서 삼백 미터쯤 더 들어가면 나오는 공원 정문 앞 음식점과 상점들은 신식 건물에 간이 분수대까지 설치해놓아 돈 쓰기 딱 좋은 곳이다. 그래서 자가용 타고 가족 나들이 온 사람들, 무슨 무슨 계나 회식하는 사람들, 머리 맞대기 좋아하는 젊은 것들이 주류이다.

그런데 유람객 중 상당수를 차지하는 중늙은이들이나 노인네들은 한 그릇에 만 원 만오천 원 하는 백숙과 쏘가리 매운탕을 손자가 끓여놓은 라면 보듯 하는 관계로 음식점은 그저 구경 삼아 쳐다보는 나무나 물과 매

"G'day," Yong-pyo said, greeting her.

"Geez...thanks to the sound of a certain jerk's mike, I can't have a good day," she answered.

"Haha, how's business?"

"What business?" she scoffed. "Everything's frozen solid. God, why is it so cold?"

"People still come in the winter, though."

Because of the park, the Secheon area was packed with people from spring—when the weather cleared and began to warm—to autumn, when the leaves changed color. Even in bitter winters like this one, cars were always coming in and out, and somber-faced teenagers continued to pass by.

Because of the fairly decent restaurants at the entrance of the park, it seemed like Secheon Corner, looking always on the verge of collapse, had been pushed into the shadows by the march of progress. However, that couldn't be further from the truth.

The restaurants and shops in front of the park's main entrance, about 300 meters past Secheon Corner, were the perfect place to spend money. The area even boasted a fountain amongst the new buildings. As such, the establishments drew families on outings, employees attending such-and-

한가지였다. 엉덩이 붙일 마땅한 곳 없는 그들에게 더없이 좋은 곳이 한갓지고 값 헐한 세천상회 마루였다. 옛적 점방 수준이라 우선 막걸리 한 되 받아놓으면 김치는 기본 안주이고 나들이 행차에 김치 쪼가리가 웬말인가 싶으면 포도나 복숭아 깡통 하나 열어놓으면 되니 취하기 편하고 놀기 좋아 머리카락으로 나이를 내보이는 이들로 언제나 북적대는 곳이다. 세천상회가 실속있는 알짜라는 것도 뜬소문만은 아닐 것이다.

용표는 지난 가을 처음 트럭 몰고 왔을 때를 기억하고 있다. 널찍한 상회 앞 공터에서 윷놀이가 한창인데 보아하니 따로 마시던 두 패가 우연히 어울린 모양이었다. 개다, 걸이다 술 오른 흰머리들이 왁자지껄하는데 판돈이 만만찮았다. 이긴 패에서 만 원짜리를 흔들며 맥주를 대령하라고 호통이었고 안주도 불기운에 등이 오그라진 오징어였다. 이를테면 공터와 돗자리, 윷이 가게 밑천인 셈이었다.

"토옹 읎어."

"에이, 아점니댁 장사 잘되기로 소문났는디."

"암튼 스무 개만 줘."

그는 계란 스무 개를 싸주고 이천 원을 받고 나서 사

such a company's staff dinner, and young people who wanted to meet up.

However, to the middle-aged or elderly, who made up a good portion of visitors, the restaurants and their boiled meat and fish stews, 10,000 or 15,000 *won* a bowl, were no different from the trees or streams that attracted tourists, because they were as uninterested in them as in the instant noodles their grandchildren would make for themselves. For these older customers, who wanted a nice spot to park their rear ends, there was no better place than the floor of the cheap, quiet Secheon Corner. It was an old-fashioned eatery, so the first thing you could expect was *makgeolli,* with kimchi as the side-dish, and if the tourists weren't big on picking at kimchi, they could crack open cans of grapes or peaches. It was a comfortable place to drink and be merry, a place that bustled with folks whose age showed in their hair. Secheon Corner's reputation as a go-to place with real appeal was no groundless rumor.

Yong-pyo thought back to the first time he came here in a truck last autumn. In the vacant lot in front of the wide store, two separate drinking groups were deep in a game of *yut*, to all appear-

백 원을 거슬러준다. 가게에 주는 도매값이다. 아줌마
는 추워, 아이구 추워, 하며 돌아가고 용표는 어제 틀었
던 오서방 메들리를 꺼내고 현철 테이프를 건다.

손대면 토옥 하고 터질 것만 같은 그대 봉선화라 부
르으으리.

동네 분위기를 보아 노래를 트는 것도 일종의 판매
전략이다.

봉선화 연정이 끝나고 싫다 싫어로 넘어가는데도 손
님이 없다. 차를 몰아 마을 안으로 들어간다. 세천상회
담벼락, 감나무, 탱자나무, 벚나무 울타리를 지나자 구
장집이 나타난다. 동네 초입에서부터 들려오던 개 짖는
소리는 바로 이 집에서 나고 있었다.

"아, 소리 점 낮춰."

마른 담쟁이덩굴이 엉성하게 우거진 돌담 위로 털벙
거지를 얹어놓은 늙은 얼굴이 나타났다. 구장이다. 볼
륨을 낮추고 차에서 내린다.

건성 인사를 나누고 울 안 풍경을 바라본 용표는 그
냥 갈 수 없다는 판단을 한다. 메마른 햇살을 잔뜩 안은
구장집 마당에는 구경하기에 꽤 괜찮은 장면이 펼쳐지
고 있다.

ances getting along well. "*It's a gae, it's a geol!*" the grey-haired players had roared, thoroughly drunk. The prize pot had been considerable. The winning team had barked orders for more beer, waving 10,000-*won* bills, and there had been a side dish of squid, warped from the heat of the fire. You could say that the vacant lot, wicker mats, and games of *yut* helped fund the store.

"No one comes around these days," the woman complained.

"Hey now, the word is that your place is bringing in good business."

"Whatever—just give me twenty of 'em."

He wrapped up twenty eggs, and after receiving 2,000 *won*, gave the woman her 400 *won* change. This was the wholesale price he offered business-es. The woman went back inside, muttering complaints about the cold, and Yong-pyo took out the O Seobang medley he'd been listening to yesterday and replaced it with a Hyeon Cheol tape.

"A blossom that would burst when I touch you, that's what you are~"

Picking the right music to go with the neighborhood was also a sort of sales strategy.

"Garden Balsam Romance" ended, but even after

구장집 누렁이가 발정이 나 검둥이가 외입꾼으로 초청이 됐는데 문제가 있는 모양이다. 순순히 뒤를 대주는 누렁이에 비해 검둥이의 덩치가 두 배는 커 서로가 원하는데도 결합이 잘 되지가 않는 것이다. 셰퍼드 잡종이 분명한 검둥이는 누렁이 등을 올라타 안간힘을 쓰며 방아질을 하는데 탄착점보다 조준점이 한 뼘은 위다. 한동안 기를 쓰던 놈은 슬며시 내려와 헐떡거리며 혀를 빼어문다. 마음대로 성사가 안 돼 안타까워하는 모습이지만 정작 속이 타는 사람은 구장이다.

눈을 가늘게 뜨고 생담배만 태우던 구장이 용표를 흘끗 쳐다보고는 멀리 꽁초를 퉁겼다. 검둥이는 재차 시도를 하지만 매 일반이다.

"대줘도 못 허냐 이 등신아. 거기는 똥구멍이잖어."

보다 못한 구장이 다가가 검둥이 아랫도리에 손을 뻗치자 놈은 다리를 뒤틀며 낑낑거린다. 방해하지 말라는 눈빛이 또렷하다. 개도 저런 눈빛을 할 수 있구나, 용표는 속으로 놀랐다.

"가만 있어, 이 등신 같은 새끼야."

그러나 도무지 싫다고 낑낑거리며 다리를 비튼다.

"뭐햐."

he passed through the neighbourhood, still no customers appeared. He drove into the village. Right past the wall of Secheon Corner and the hedges of persimmon trees, mandarin trees, and cherry trees, was the house of the district head. A dog's barking, heard all the way from the edge of the neighbourhood, was coming from this place.

"Hey, lower the volume, will ya?"

A wrinkled face under a fur-lined military-style hat appeared over a stone wall that was crawling with a dense mess of dried vines. It was the district head. Yong-pyo turned down the music and got out of the truck.

Yong-pyo greeted the man half-heartedly and surveyed the area. He couldn't just leave now, Yong-pyo decided. In the barren yard, enveloped in sunlight, an eyebrow-raising scene was unfolding.

There seemed to be a bit of a problem going on with a pair of dogs. A yellow dog in heat was propositioning a black dog, submissively offering her rear end. But the black dog was twice her size, and enthusiastic though they were, they hadn't yet managed to couple. The black dog, who clearly had some shepherd blood, had mounted the other

그때 사립문 밖에서 말소리가 들려왔다. 구장 또래인 반백에 주름살이다.

"이, 댕겨가는 겨?"

"그려, 뭐햐?"

"이 등신 같은 게 지 집도 못 찾아 맞춰줄려구 허는디 이 지랄이잖어. 내 참."

"ᄒᄒ, 욕보는구먼."

"가만 있으라니까."

구장이 신경질을 내며 검둥이 엉덩짝을 내갈겼다. 깽. 놈은 비명을 지르면서도 도망가지는 않았다.

"안 되면 대신햐."

못 들은 척 그저 지나가면 그만인데 용표는 자신도 모르게 낄낄 웃고 말았다. 그는 가늘게 누운 구장의 눈초리가 자신을 향해 있다는 사실을 깨달았다.

"낼 모리 늙어 죽을 게 당췌 끝까지 으른 티는 못 내는구먼. 할 소리 못할 소리 구분도 못햐?"

친구에게 한마디 쏘아붙이고 이쪽으로 돌아온 구장의 찌그러진 얼굴이 너 잘 만났다는 표정이다.

"계란 팔러 왔으믄 휘딱 팔구 갈 것이지 넘 삽짝은 왜 넘보고 지랄이여?"

dog and was thrusting with great effort, but his target was a hand's width above where he was actually making contact.

Although the sight of them failing at their goal was pitiful, the one agonizing the most was the district head. Holding a cigarette between his fingers without smoking it, he stole a glance at Yongpyo through narrowed eyes and flicked the butt far away. Meanwhile, the black dog made another attempt at entry but came up empty.

"She's offering, but you still can't do it, you moron. I'm tellin' ya, that's the shit-hole." Unable to watch any longer, the district head stuck his hands out under the black dog, who immediately complained, whining as his legs buckled. The dog's expression was a plain warning not to interfere. So, dogs can also have that kind of expression, Yongpyo mused, surprised.

"Stay still, you dumb bastard."

The dog just wouldn't have any of it, whimpering and squirming.

"What's going on?" a voice called from outside the wicker gate. The voice belonged to a man who in terms of grey hair and wrinkles could have been about the same age as the district head.

아차 싶다.

"그게 아닌디유. 저 뭐시냐 하믄."

"재수 읎는 소리 지껄이지 말구 얼른 눈앞에서 사라
져."

아무래도 잘못 걸린 듯싶다. 용표처럼 현지인들과의
안면 확보가 수익에 영향을 주는 직업을 가진 사람일수
록 더욱 좋은 인상을 남겨줘야 하지 않는가. 슬그머니
고개를 내린다.

"싸가지 읎이."

구장의 마무리 인사가 담벼락을 넘어왔다. 가슴이 확
달아오르는 것을 눌러 참는다. 그놈의 웃음 때문이다,
라는 나름의 반성이 있었기 때문이다. 그렇게 다짐을
했건만 세 가지 조심 중에 첫 번째인 입조심을 어긴 거
였다.

현철 혼자 부지런히 노래하고 있는 차로 다가가자 조
무래기들이 우르르 몰려 달아난다. 문을 열려다가 이상
한 느낌이 들어 짐칸을 살펴보니 아니나 다를까 맨 위
쪽 계란판에 있는 대란 두 개가 박살나 있다. 연 꼭지가
곤두박질 친 모양이다. 아이들은 이쪽을 돌아보면서도
벌써 저만치 달음박질치고 있다. 이런 싸가지, 하다가

"Hey, just dropping by?" the district head greeted him.

"Yeah, what's up?" the other man said.

"This dumbass dog can't find its way home and is losing it trying to hook up. My God..." the district head shook his head.

"Sounds like you're having as hard a time as the dog," the friend chuckled.

The district head slapped the dog's rump. "I told you to stay still," he roared. The mutt yelped, but didn't run.

"If that doesn't work, you should just take his place," the other man said.

Yong-pyo could have turned a deaf ear and kept walking, but couldn't help snickering. And that's when he realized the district head was aiming an angry gaze in his direction.

"You're about to drop dead, you old geezer, and you still don't know how to talk in public?" the district head spat at his friend while still facing Yong-pyo, his expression reading, *perfect timing.*

"If you came to sell eggs, then sell them and get a move on. Why are you sticking your nose into other people's business?"

Jesus!

입을 틀어막는다. 구장의 노여운 얼굴이 담벼락 위에 걸쳐져 있었다,

용표가 새벽부터 조심을 다짐했던 이유는 바로 여동생 때문이었다. 용순이가 아들 아람이를 질질 끌다시피 하고 들이닥친 것은 어제 늦은 밤이었다. 선 채로 냉수를 벌컥벌컥 들이킨 용순은 퍼질러 앉기가 무섭게 푸념부터 내놓았다.

"나 그 인간하고는 더 못 살어."

"또 싸웠니?"

선잠이 들었다 깬 그가 볼이 언 조카를 끌어당기며 물었다.

"이젠 증말 끝장이여. 갈라설 거야."

입술을 부르르 떨고 있는 용순의 눈가에 얼핏 피멍이 비쳤다. 없는 집 자식들로 만나 아직 식도 못 올렸지만 그래도 아들 낳고 보란 듯 살았는데 요즘 들어 툭하면 싸움이었다.

"아람이는 워칙허구."

"몰러. 지가 깡패야 뭐야. 철근쟁이 주먹자랑을 왜 집구석에서 하는 거야."

"좀 진정 좀 허구. 오늘은 왜 싸웠는지 말부터 해봐."

"What are you talking about? What am I doing?"

"Stop whining and get lost!"

Somehow Yong-pyo felt mistreated. On the other hand, shouldn't people like him leave a better impression on the locals, good relations with whom could fatten his income? Yong-pyo discreetly lowered his head.

"You bastard. Bringing bad luck on all of us." The district head hurled his parting insult at Yong-pyo over the wall. Yong-pyo suppressed the rage that leapt up in his chest, ruing the fact that it was his own laugh that had started it all. He had violated the first of the three rules he had resolved to follow: watch your mouth.

A flock of children approached the truck, which was still streaming Hyeon Cheol's lone diligent voice, only to scamper away. Struck by suspicion, Yong-pyo opened the rear gate and checked the trunk bed. Sure enough, two eggs in the uppermost carton had been smashed. The kids' kite must have done a nose-dive. The children were running away, looking back in his direction all the while. "Those brats," Yong-pyo said before clamping his mouth shut. The district head's angry face still hovered right above the wall.

"아, 몰러."

"모른다니?"

"가뜩이나 새끼도 커가는데 돈 벌 궁리는 않구 술에 노름에."

제 어미의 말에 주눅이 들었는지 울지도 않고 퉁방울 같은 눈만 슬금슬금 굴리고 있는 아람이에게 이불을 덮어주며 용표는 휘유, 한숨을 내쉬었다.

"요즘 경기가 웬만해야지."

그는 용순과 매제의 싸움에 나설 계제가 아니었다. 쉽게 말해 여동생을 이렇게 만들어놓은 매제를 따끔하게 야단칠 형편이 못 된다는 것인데 이유는 트럭을 살 때 용순에게는 비밀로 하고 꾼 삼백만 원을 아직 못 갚고 있기 때문이었다. 내막도 모르고 제 서방의 손버릇 좀 고쳐달라고 하는 시위도 시위인데다 피멍 든 얼굴을 볼 때의 서운함 또한 이루 말할 수 없지만 매제의 입이 무거운 것에 감사하고 있는 터라 번번이 큰소리 한번 못 내고 있는 터였다.

노총각 오빠 단칸방을 찾아든 용순은 한바탕 사설에 눈물 콧물까지 곁들이다가 그대로 누워버렸다.

"그렇다구 여기서 자면 워칙허냐. 그래도 서방이구 애

The reason Yong-pyo had made those resolutions that morning was for the sake of his younger sister. Late last night Yong-sun had dropped in without warning, practically dragging her daughter A-ram with her. She had stood there downing water until she flopped onto the floor, whereupon she unleashed a volley of complaints.

"I can't live with that man anymore."

"You guys fought again?" he had asked, pulling his niece, whose cheeks were frozen, closer.

"This time it's really over. We're breaking up," she had said, her lips trembling, one eye sporting a shiny bruise.

She and her husband had come from families so poor they couldn't afford a wedding ceremony. Still, they were raising a family and had nothing to be ashamed of. Lately, however, they had been fighting.

"What's going to happen to A-ram?"

"I don't know. He's a goddamn bully. Why's he showing off his fists at home?"

"Please, calm down. Start with why you guys fought today."

"Ugh, I don't know."

"You don't know?"

아빤데 안 찾겠니, 얼른 가."

달래고 얼렀지만 용순은 아람이를 껴안고 잠이 들어 버렸다. 매제는 전화를 받지 않았다. 아랫목을 내주고 윗목에서 새우잠을 자던 그는 새벽에 한 번 더 깨야 했다. 매제가 술이 떡이 되어 찾아온 거였다.

"이 빌어먹을 년. 멀리 가지도 못하면서 뛰쳐나가."

발을 들여놓기가 무섭게 한바탕 호통이었다. 삽시간에 용순의 머리채가 잡혔다. 용표는 부랴부랴 말리고 조카는 불에 덴 듯 울어댔다.

"어디 한번 죽어봐라."

"오빠, 나 좀 살려주, 악."

"이봐, 박 서방 참어."

때 아닌 난리였다. 주전자가 엎어지고 밥통이 뒤집혔고 쏟아진 밥이 밟혀 빈대떡이 되었다.

"지금이 몇 신디 이 난리여. 한두 살 먹은 애덜두 아니구. 아, 싸울라믄 날이나 새구 싸워."

주인집 영감의 불호령이 떨어져도 한참이나 가던 난리는 매제가 용표의 발에 걸려 넘어지면서 끝이 났다.

용표는 새록새록 눈앞에 그려지는 장면을 애써 지운다. 새벽부터 그 지경이었으니 일진이 좋을 리 없다. 그

"On top of our kid getting bigger, he doesn't think about making money—all he cares about is booze and gambling."

Yong-pyo sighed, then pulled the blanket over A-ram, who, perhaps intimidated by her mother's words, was looking around, goggle-eyed.

"The economy is bad these days," he observed.

But he was in no position to butt into Yong-sun and her husband's argument. To put it simply, he couldn't give his brother-in-law a scolding for getting his sister all riled up, the reason being that he was still unable to pay back the 3 million *won* he'd borrowed from him, unbeknownst to her, to buy his truck. On top of her pleas to help cure her husband of his wife-beating proclivities and her ignorance of the financial matter involving her brother and her husband, the sadness he felt when he looked at her bruised face was beyond description—but, grateful to his brother-in-law for keeping his mouth shut about the loan, not once could he raise his voice in consternation.

Having rushed into her bachelor big brother's room, and burst out crying, tears running from her eyes and nose, Yong-sun simply lay there motionless.

저 오늘 하루 눈 질끈 감고 쓸데없는 말 않고 손도 아끼고 해서 무탈하게 넘어 가야겠다, 다시 한 번 매듭을 만든다. 그러고 보니 속이 출출하다. 아침도 거른데다 어느덧 점심때가 다 되었다.

차는 옥천에 들어선다. 그는 종종 들리는 대성반점 문을 열고 들어가 짬뽕을 시킨다.

"병아리 아빠, 우리 계란 떨어졌는데 두 판만 줘요."

뚱뚱한 홀 아가씨가 농담조를 붙여왔다. 여느 때 같으면 서로 농을 주고받기도 할 텐데 그저 고개만 끄덕여 계란을 갖다주고 근처의 신문을 펴들었다.

"무공해 유정란이 왔습니다. 인위적인 인공 절차를 거치지 않은 순수 무공해 유정란이 왔습니다. 위생 시설이 완벽하게 갖추어진 신생 농장에서 방금 생산된 천연 유정란이 왔습니다."

아파트 입구에 코트를 어깨에 걸친 여자들이 하나둘씩 나타난다.

"싱싱해요?"

"그럼요. 오늘 받아온 것이에요."

역시 아파트에는 유정란이나 효소란이 잘 나간다. 담아줄 것 담아주고 돈 받아 거슬러줄 것 거슬러주고 하

"Even so, how can you sleep here? He's still your husband and your child's father—you think he won't come looking for you? Go, hurry!" Yong-pyo had pleaded, but Yong-sun had already fallen asleep with A-ram in her arms.

Her husband hadn't answer Yong-pyo's call. Instead, Yong-pyo, curled up on the cooler part of the heated floor, having given the warmest spot to his sister and niece, had been roused once more, early the next morning. It was his brother-in-law, dead drunk, looking for his wife.

"Cheap whore. She can't even get anywhere but still runs away from home." In an angry fit he stomped in and grabbed Yong-sun by her hair. Yong-pyo had rushed between them as A-ram began caterwauling as if she'd been dipped in fire.

"Go to hell."

"Yong-pyo, save me—please!" she'd screeched.

"Hey! Control yourself, brother-in-law."

It had been an ill-timed commotion. The kettle had been knocked over, the pot of rice capsized, and the scattered rice flattened underfoot, looking like *bindaetteok* in the end.

"Do you have any idea what time it is, making a fuss like this? You aren't toddlers. If you want to

고 있는데,

"어째 싱싱하지 못한 것 같다."

엇조가 튀어나온 곳을 보니 안경 쓴 단발머리이다.

"오늘 새벽에 받아온 건디 뭔 말씀이래요?"

용표는 단발머리를 기억하고 있다. 유정란 코스를 개척하기 위해 이 아파트 단지에 들어오던 첫날부터 까탈을 부리던 여자였다. 계란을 사든 안 사든 그냥 가는 법 없는데다 서비스 차원에서 하나씩 줬던 바가지도 이 핑계 저 이유로 세 개나 뜯어간 위인이었다.

"아니이. 때깔이 좀 그래서······"

"뭐가요. 좋기만 하구만."

"요전엣 것도 신선하지 않던데."

"아닐 낀디······"

"노른자가 탱탱하지 않던데."

참자. 용표는 고개를 다른 손님에게 돌렸다.

"어머, 이건 깨졌네. 큰놈이라 아저씨가 먹고 그냥 됐나봐."

짐칸 맨 앞쪽 한 줄에 나란히 서 있는 유정란 더미 중에서 고객들 쪽, 그것도 단발머리 바로 앞 판에 구멍이 나 있는 대란이 보였다. 흘러내린 내용물이 하얗게 굳

squabble, at least let the sun rise first," Yong-pyo's landlord reprimanded them. Nevertheless, the argument ended only when the brother-in-law tripped over Yong-pyo's foot.

Yong-pyo tried to wipe out these scenes, which kept popping up one after another in his mind. Having started the day with such a calamity, he was convinced he was out of luck. *Just today. I just have to keep my eyes shut, keep my mouth shut, keep my hands to myself, and get through the day without any more problems*, Yong-pyo thought to himself, re-affirming his resolution. Come to think of it, I'm a little hungry, he realized. He had skipped breakfast, and now lunchtime had snuck up on him.

He drove into Okcheon, to the Daeseong Eatery, where he ordered a bowl of spicy seafood noodles.

"Chick daddy, we ran out of eggs. Give us two cartons please," the serving girl joked as she approached him. Normally, he would have bantered with her, but today he just nodded, fetched her the eggs, and spread open up the local newspaper.

"Eco-friendly organic eggs! Get your uncontaminated, organic eggs—no artificial procedures involved! Natural eggs fresh from Sinsaeng Farms,

어 햇볕이 반사되고 있었다. 세천동 아이들이 깨뜨린 것인데 교환한다는 것을 잊었던 것이다.

이 씨. 그는 깨진 놈을 꺼내 무녀리들만 모아두는 판에 치웠다. 그 판에는 옆구리가 터진 놈, 온몸이 세로로 쩍 갈라진 놈, 아예 박살이 난 놈들이 제각기 눕거나 찌부러진 채 터져나온 흰자위로 반들거렸다. 여자 두엇이 자리를 떴다. 용표는 오장육부 중 하나가 떨어져나가는 것 같았다.

단발머리는 맨 마지막까지 남아 고르고 고른 유정란 스무 개를 바가지에 담아달라고 했다. 참자. 이번이 마지막이다. 그는 입을 꾹 다물고 빨간 바가지에 계란을 담아준다.

확실히 사람이란 게 마음이 비틀어지면 주위 일들도 덩달아 꼬이는 법이다. 매제는 그렇게 나자빠져 코를 골았다. 울어제끼는 아람이를 달래 재우고 그는 새벽 담배를 태웠다. 한동안 흐느끼던 용순이 코 막힌 소리로,

"오빠, 저이가 저래. 원래 그런 사람이 아닌데……"

하는데 저녁과는 달리 말에 힘이 없었다. 용표는 고개를 끄덕거렸다.

prepared to perfection in sanitary facilities!"

Girls appeared at the entrance to the apartment complex, some alone and others with friends, coats thrown over their shoulders.

"Are they fresh?"

"You bet, farm-fresh!"

Organic eggs and enzyme-modified eggs really did sell well to apartment dwellers, after all. He handed out the orders, took payment, and was making change when—

"Well, they don't look it."

He followed the voice and saw a woman with bobbed hair and glasses.

"What are you talking about? I got 'em just this morning."

Ah yes, Bobbed Hair. She'd been a nuisance ever since he'd first arrived at the apartment complex trying to find a new market for his organic eggs. On top of not leaving him alone, waffling between buying or not buying eggs, she was a clever fox who, even when it came to the plastic bowl he gave out as a bonus, would wheedle two or three more bowls from him, citing this or that reason or excuse.

"No, no. Just look at the color..."

"철근 일 그만하고 같이 장사라도 해야겠어."

장사라는 말에 가슴이 뜨끔했다.

"아무리 겨울이라지만 일이 그렇게 읎대?"

"엑스포 헐 때까지는 괜찮았는데…… 일도 별루 읎는
데다 이번 현장 끝난 것두 업주헌티서 돈이 안 나온대."

"머리나 좀 빗어라."

용순은 산발된 머리카락을 다듬었다. 아침이 밝고 콩
나물을 사러 가는 용순이 뒷모습을 바라보다가 그는 차
에 시동을 걸었다.

좋아지겠지. 그렇게 생각했다. 모든 게 생각하기 나름
이었다. 아파트 각 동을 대충 돌아 빠져나오다가 집에
전화를 했다. 띠리리릭 띠리리릭. 집도 받지 않고 용순
네도 받지 않는다. 어디 간 걸까. 별일 없겠지. 시장에
갔거나 유치원 간 아이 마중하러 갔겠지, 싶다.

식을 올리면 괜찮을려나. 내가 얼른 돈을 벌어 빚도
갚고 식도 올려주고 해야 할 텐데, 하다가 픽 웃는다. 용
순에게 그 말을 건네면 오빠부터 빨랑 좋은 여자 얻어
결혼해야 한다고 뻗댈 게 뻔하기 때문이었다. 운동복
차림의 남자를 마지막으로 시동을 건다. 어차피 쪼그라
든 하루, 매상 따윈 신경 쓰지 말고 어디 산 좋은 동네나

"What? I only sell good eggs."

"The ones the other day didn't look fresh, either."

"I'm telling you, that's not the case..."

"The yolks weren't bouncy."

Just bear with it. Yong-pyo turned towards other customers.

"Oh my, these are cracked. Look how big they are. You must have eaten them and forgot to pick up after yourself."

In the carton right in front of the customers, including Bobbed Hair, amongst the stacks of neatly lined eggs at the front of the truck's bed, were several large broken eggs. The insides, which had leaked out, were hardening into a white mess and reflected the sunlight. He had forgotten to replace the ones smashed by the Secheon kids. *Dammit.* He took out the broken ones and put them into the carton reserved for bad eggs. Eggs that had their sides shattered. Eggs that were cracked from end to end. And eggs that had been smashed. They were each either lying there or, having been crushed, were glistening in their erupted whites. A couple of girls left. Yong-pyo felt a surge in his guts.

Bobbed Hair, the last person left, selected her

돌아다니며 하루해를 저물리기로 작정한다.

하늘은 저만치 홀로 높아 시퍼런 기운이 더욱 심하다. 긴 겨울잠에 들어간 논과 밭 두덕에 잡풀이 하얗게 말랐다. 옷을 벗은 산은 엉성하여 을씨년스럽다.

몇몇 동네를 돌았으나 처음부터 포기한 마음이어서인지 정말 손님이 없다. 젓가락 같은 감나무 가지들이 잔뜩 하늘을 찌르고 있는 동네를 벗어나 얼음 밑으로 물방울을 만들며 흐르는 냇가 다리 위에 차를 세우고 내린 용표는 사람 눈 안 가는 곳을 골라 바지춤을 내렸다. 산비둘기 한 마리가 인기척에 놀라 푸다닥 날아오른다. 누렇게 퍼지는 오줌발을 보며 이 오줌발처럼 모든 게 술술 풀렸으면 좋겠구나 생각을 했다. 어흐으, 몸을 부르르 떨고는 올라오는데 누군가 멀뚱히 자신을 바라보고 있음을 알았다. 상체를 반듯이 세우지 못하고 앞뒤로 흔들거리고 있는 짧은 머리이다.

"앗씨, 대전 나가요?"

"그려."

"대전까지 태워쥬. 버스 놓쳤슈."

짧은 머리 밑으로 면도 자국이 시퍼렇다. 낮술을 거나하게 걸쳤는지 낯바닥과 눈알에 온통 붉은 물이 들었고

eggs and asked for the twenty she had chosen to be put into a plastic bowl. *Hang in there. This is the last time.* He clamped his lips shut and put the eggs into a red plastic bowl.

In most cases, when a heavy rain cloud hangs overhead, the rain will cover everything in its immediate vicinity. Yong-pyo's brother-in-law had passed out, his snoring filling the room. Yong-pyo had soothed the wailing A-ram, putting her to sleep, before lighting his first cigarette of the day.

"Look at him. He wasn't like that before," Yong-sun had sniffed, her nose heavily congested. She had been weeping a good while, but unlike her words the evening before, they sounded half-hearted. Yong-pyo had shaken his head.

"He'll have to quit working construction and go into business with me," she'd said.

The sound of the word "business" had pricked at his conscience.

"I know it's winter, but is it really that hard to find construction work?" he had asked.

"It was fine up until the Expo...but now, not only is there no work, the boss from the last site hasn't even paid us yet."

"Just go brush your hair."

잠바도 잔뜩 구겨져 있다.

"그려, 타봐."

이런 공양은 종종 있었다. 사람들이 트럭이라 저어하고 계란차라 속도를 우습게 아는 경향이 있지만 일단 손을 들어 방향만 같으면 용표는 되도록 동승하기를 꺼려하지 않았다.

"휴가 나왔는감?"

구불거리는 신작로를 빠져나오며 인사차 물었다.

"휴가요?"

대답 대신 끄덕거려주니

"해병 잡는 방바리요."

하면서 고개를 뻣뻣이 세운다. 술냄새와 입냄새가 확 끼쳐오는데 붉게 충혈된 눈빛이 감히 도전적이다. 뭐 이런 게 있나 싶지만 모르는 척한다.

"방바리 태워 기분 나빠?"

"어지간히 취했구만."

"예. 좆 겉은 고참놈이 제대를 했는데 그 집서 한잔했쥬."

상판이 막돼먹게 생긴 것 같지는 않은데 술기가 머릿속을 파고들었는지 아니면 그 뭣 같다는 고참이랑 한바

Yong-sun raked her fingers through her disheveled tresses. The sky grew brighter. Yong-pyo had watched his sister's back recede as she left to go buy bean sprouts, then started up his truck.

It'll get better, he thought. Everything depended on how he thought about it. He threaded his way through the apartment complex and then called home. *Dooooot doooooot.* No one was picking up at home or at Yong-sun's place. Where could she have gone? It probably wasn't a big deal. She must have gone to the market or to the daycare to pick up A-ram.

I wonder if things will get better if they have a ceremony. I'll scrounge up some cash, pay them back, and hold a ceremony for them, Yong-pyo thought, chuckling to himself. Though if he ever mentioned this to Yong-sun, she would of course insist that he first find himself a nice woman and get hitched. He finished up with his last customer, a man in exercise wear, and got back in his truck. He decided not to think about sales and such, as it didn't seem like a good day for him, and instead to just spend the rest of the waning day driving around the vicinity, admiring the fine mountain view.

The sky was all the more lofty that day, an in-

탕 드잡이를 했는지 불화 같은 기운이 뻗쳐나온다.

"이봐, 해병 잡는 방바리 아저씨. 넘의 차 공짜로 탔으면 얌전히 있어야지."

그는 어린 방위의 술주정이 되려 귀엽기까지 했다. 매사를 좋게 생각하고 각종 조심을 하자는 다짐 때문에 그럴지도 모르지만 아무튼 성깔 없는 사람이 어디 있겠는가, 그도 여차하면 술을 찾고 취했다 하면 싸울 상대를 고르던 세월이 있었다. 젊다는 게 벼슬은 아니지만 그러나 그 나이 때는 기운이 승할 수밖에 없고 또 때때로 속으로 웅숭그리지 못하고 삐져나올 때도 있지 않나 싶어 인상을 구기지는 않았다. 그러나 수그러질 기세가 아니다.

"그 좆 같은 놈 제대 파티를 어저께 했는디 좆도, 그 새끼헌티 당헌 걸 갚을려고 오늘까지 기둘렀슈."

"그래서?"

"한판 붙었쥬. 씨팔놈, 쌈도 좆도 못하는 게 고참이라고…… 허이구."

"그래 이겼어?"

"내가 이기긴 이긴 것 같은디 아구창 이빨이 나갔나 왜 이리 아퍼."

tense, brilliant blue. In the sloping fields and paddies, which had lapsed into their long winter hibernation, the stalks had dried, turning white. The mountains, which had shed their cloaks, looked sparse and desolate.

He circled several neighborhoods, but perhaps because he had already called it a day when he had started this latest route, there was not a single customer. He left the last neighborhood, the chopstick-like branches of its persimmon trees piercing the sky, and stopped the truck on a small bridge over a brook that ran beneath a layer of ice. As he climbed down from the truck, he picked a place hidden from prying eyes and pulled down the waist of his pants. Startled by his presence, a wood pigeon took off fluttering into the air. He looked at his stream of bright yellow urine and wished that he could get rid of all his other problems just as easily. He gave himself a shake and was climbing back onto his truck when he noticed a young man with short hair, bent over double and rocking back and forth, staring blankly at him.

"Hey mister, are you going to Daejeon?" the young man asked.

"Yeah," Yong-pyo said.

"맞기도 했구먼."

"씨펄, 안 맞고 하는 쌈 있슈? 알믄 갈쳐주. 날마다 하게."

용표는 담배를 물었다.

"하나 줘유."

그것 참, 한 개비를 건넸다.

"씨팔, 라이타가 어디 갔나."

방위병은 호주머니마다 뒤지기 시작했다. 내친김이라 불까지 붙여주었다. 차는 큰길로 접어든다.

"아, 씨…… 음, 으으으음."

가래를 뽑아올리는지 힘주어 신음을 내뱉는 방위병은 몸을 창 쪽으로 완전히 구부리고 있다. 눈알은 개개 풀려 있고 침을 고여 문 입을 연신 우물거린다. 허참, 기가 막혀서. 헛웃음을 흘리다 깜짝 놀랐다. 힘없이 늘어뜨린 손아귀의 담뱃불이 시트를 태우고 있는 것이 아닌가.

"야, 임마."

곧바로 손을 뻗어 담배를 털어냈다. 그러나 가랑이 사이 시트에는 벌써 손가락만한 구멍이 나 있었다. 그러는 사이 차는 갓길 쪽으로 휘어졌고 아이고, 놀란 나머

"Gimme a ride there, will ya? I missed the bus."

Under his cropped hair, the young man had an angry-looking shaving scar. He seemed to have been drinking; his face was flushed, his eyes bloodshot, and his jacket thoroughly wrinkled.

"Sure, hop in."

Every now and then, he would help people out like this. Even though people tended to be wary of trucks and often ridiculed his truck's speed because of its load of eggs, if they held out their hand and were travelling in the same direction, Yong-pyo was not at all reluctant to give them a ride.

"You on leave?" he asked by way of greeting as he left the winding main road.

"On leave?" the young man repeated the question.

Yong-pyo nodded.

"No, I'm in the National Guard, stronger than a marine."

The young man held his head up stiffly. A blast of his breath and the stench of liquor hit Yong-pyo full in the face. The man stared at him defiantly. *Who really was this guy?* Yong-pyo ignored him.

"You don't like driving a national guardsman around?"

지 운전대를 반대로 꺾었다. 휘청. 중앙선을 스치고 가까스로 중심을 잡았다. 빠아앙. 맞은편에서 달려오던 덤프트럭이 경적을 울리며 부딪칠 듯 스쳐갔다. 한순간 식은땀이 쭈욱 흘렀다. 쏠리는 기운에 따라 차가 사정없이 휘청거렸는데도 방위병은 이미 딴 세계로 가 있다.

"아이 씨, 뭐야."

"이 자식이 증말."

얼른 고개 돌려 짐칸 계란판을 살핀 용표의 눈초리가 올라갔다. 계란판은 넘어지지는 않았으나 오와 열이 흐트러져 있었다.

"욕하지 마, 짜샤. 나도 고참이여…… 음, 음."

그리고는 몸을 눕혀버렸다. 가슴속에 불기둥 같은 게 솟아올랐다.

"내려, 이 새끼야."

방위병은 잠들었는지 요동도 하지 않았다. 정말 내 재수가 없으려니까. 혼자 숨을 몰아쉬며 자신에게 물어본다. 오늘은 무슨 일진이 이렇지? 그렇게 조심했는데 도대체 왜 이러는 거야? 이유를 알 수 없다. 창문을 열었다. 차가운 바람이 몰아쳐 들어오자 정신이 조금 새로워졌다. 그때였다. 우욱, 웩.

"You look pretty drunk."

"Mmm-hmm. This dickhead was discharged so we had a drink at his place."

The young man didn't look especially nasty, but perhaps because of the alcohol worming its way into his brain, or perhaps because he had gotten into a scuffle with that dickhead discharged that day, he was emanating a fiery anger.

"Look here, Mister National Guardsman, if you're going to hitch a ride with someone, shouldn't you at least try to behave yourself?"

The young guardsman was drunk in a cute way, thought Yong-pyo, resolving once again to think well of everything and to mind his manners. In any case, he told himself, who doesn't have a few crabby fits at some point? He himself had sometimes gotten drunk and, in a drinking frame of mind, picked fights. Being young doesn't put you on top of the world, but when you are young, you can't keep things inside yourself and you lash out instead. Thinking such thoughts, Yong-pyo couldn't look down on the young man. However, the young man's anger didn't seem to go away.

"That bastard that put on the party yesterday—I'd been waiting until today to get my revenge on that

접혀져 있던 방위병이 토하기 시작했다. 용표는 막 눈앞에 나타난 주유소에 끼이익, 차를 세우고 후다닥 뛰어 조수석 문을 열고 그를 끄집어냈다. 그러나 이미 늦었다. 차 안은 물론 제 신발과 바짓가랑이까지 한바탕 분칠을 해놓고 난 다음이었다.

"뭐 이런 자식이 있어."

분명 태울 때는 이 지경이 될 정도라고 짐작되진 않았는데 따뜻한 차 안이 문제였던 모양이다.

"개새끼, 많이도 처먹었네."

한동안 주유소 벽에 기대어 앉아 있는 방위병을 노려보던 용표는 긴 한숨을 내쉬고 주유소 수돗가로 차를 몰았다. 보여주기 뭣한 거라 부랴부랴 꼭지를 틀고 차 안을 씻어냈다. 주유원이 나와 지켜보고 있었으므로 되도록 태연하게 호스질을 했지만 낯이 뜨겁다. 한참을 그렇게 씻어내고 마당까지 청소하고 나서 보니 방위병이 저만치 승강장에서 막 버스에 오르는 것이 보인다. 쫓아가 따귀라도 한 대 올려붙이고 싶은데 버스는 부우웅 출발해버린다.

"만땅으로 채워쥬."

줄곧 곱지 않은 눈초리를 하고 있는 주유원에게 그는

dickhead."

"And?"

"We fought. That fucker, he's my superior but he can't fight or do nothin' for shit."

"So you won?

"Well, as for winning, I think I won, but why am I in pain? A tooth musta come out or somethin'."

"You must've gotten pasted."

"Fuck, what kind of fight would it be if I didn't get hit? If you know how to fight without getting hit, please teach me how. I'll fight every day."

Yong-pyo took a drag on his cigarette.

"Gimme one, will ya," the soldier demanded.

Well geez. Yong-pyo obliged.

"Shit, where did my lighter go?"

Watching the guardsman dig around in his pockets, Yong-pyo figured he might as well give him a light too. The car ambled onto the main road and the man produced a groan that sounded like he was clearing his throat.

He was bent over towards the window, eyes unfocused, and he kept mumbling through his drooling mouth.

"Unbelievable," Yong-pyo snorted and tried to smile it off. But the next moment he was utterly

웃음을 흘렸다. 정말이지 아무리 일진이 사납다고 이렇게까지 사나운가. 머릿속이 어질거리고 속까지 메스꺼워져 이제는 제가 토할 판이다.

아무래도 철저하게 그른 날이다. 그저 쉬고만 싶어졌다. 짐칸의 계란판을 다시 정리하고 나서 대전을 향해 차를 몰았다. 오늘 남은 코스는 포기다. 얼른 집에 가서 씻고 눕자. 하루 종일 그렇게 조심했는데도 이렇게 꼬이는 날은 그저 피하는 게 수다. 오늘만 날이냐. 오늘 같은 날은 노는 게 버는 거다.

정차 중인 시내버스를 추월했다. 들를 곳이 이제 없어졌기 때문에 별 생각 없이 추월용 1차선을 타고 간 게 또 하나의 사단이었다. 나지막한 언덕빼기를 넘어 막 대전 시내가 보이는 곳에 다다랐을 때였다.

"계란차는 우측으로, 계란차는 우측으로."

무심히 운전을 하던 그는 거울을 통해 그 소리가 뒤에서 따라오는 순찰차의 스피커에서 나온다는 것을 알았다.

낭패였다. 이런.

"계란차는 우측으로, 계란차는 우측으로."

뒤에서 다시 재촉하는 소리가 들려왔다. 네모 길쭉한

surprised. The cigarette in the young man's dangling hand was singeing the seat.

"Hey, you!"

Yong-pyo swiped at the cigarette, but not before a hole the size of his finger appeared in the seat, right between the guardsman's legs. In the meantime the truck was drifting toward the shoulder, and he had to yank it back the other way. This time he grazed the centre line before he was able to correct. The truck's tires squealed as a dump truck came honking from the other direction, barely missing them. Cold sweat ran down Yong-pyo's face. Although the truck was swaying wildly from the momentum, the guardsman was off in his own little world.

"Ugh, what the hell?" the guard said.

"Hey, you, fuck!"

Yong-pyo's checked the rear-view mirror for the egg cartons. They were still intact, but in complete disarray.

"Don't curse, you... I'm a senior guard, too," said the young man as he slumped over.

Yong-pyo felt a hot pillar of anger rise inside of him.

"Get out, you bastard."

순찰차 등에서 불빛이 살아 있는 듯 꼬물거린다.

"증말, 재수가 없으려니까."

차를 갓길에 세웠다. 앞에 선 순찰차 문이 열리고 몸집이 좋은 경찰이 다가와 경례를 한다.

"수고가 많으십니다. 면허증 좀 주시죠."

용표는 그러나 관록 있는 운전수였다.

"한 번만 봐주십쇼. 계속 2차선으로 오다가 시내버스 추월하느라고 그만."

그는 인상 좋아 보이게끔 웃어주면서 이 일진이라는 놈을 만날 수만 있다면 한주먹에 박살내버리겠다고 다짐했다.

"차선 위반입니다. 면허증 좀 주시죠."

"아이구, 우리같이 벌어먹고 사는 사람헌티 꼭 딱지를 떼야겠습니까. 한번 봐유. 계란 팔아서 얼마나 번다고, 그러지 말고 한 번만 봐주십쇼."

경찰은 딴청을 부리느라 고개를 뽑아 이쪽저쪽을 바라보며 손바닥만 까딱거리고 있다. 용표는 최대한 인내력을 가지고 흥정을 시작한다.

"오늘은 정말 내 일당도 못했슈. 증말이유. 오죽했으면 지금 장사 포기하고 집으로 가는 참이라니까요. 그

The soldier didn't move. Was he asleep? *I really have no luck whatsoever today, do I?* Yong-pyo took a deep breath. *What kind of luck do I have, having to deal with this kind of day? I tried so hard to keep things under control, so why on earth did today turn out this way?* There was no explaining it. He opened the window. Cool air flooded in, and he felt better—until he heard an unmistakable splatter on the floor of his truck.

The huddled guardsman retched. Yong-pyo screeched to a stop at a gas station and hurried around to the passenger side. He opened the door and dragged the man out, but it was too late. The inside of the truck, as well as his shoes and pants, were plastered with vomit.

"This guy is unbelievable."

So this was what happened when you offered a guy a ride. Was it the warm interior of his truck that had led to this mess?

"Bastard must have had a shitload to drink."

Yong-pyo glared at the guardsman, who was propped up against the wall of the gas station, then let out a long sigh. He drove up to a faucet and attempted, as unobtrusively as he could, to clean the inside of his truck. An attendant came out and

러지 말구 우리 겉은 사람헌티 인심 좀 쓰시는 게."

굽신거리는 고갯짓을 한동안 물끄러미 바라보던 경찰이 고개를 끄덕인다.

"그럼 만 원짜리로 끊어드리지."

"오늘 기름값두 못했슈."

"허참, 이 양반이."

"저기. 안전거리 미확보 하나 떼줘요."

"오천 원짜리로? 말도 안 돼. 만 원짜리로 해."

그러나 결국 경찰을 이기고 만다.

"그 양반 참…… 그러면 이렇게 하지. 그냥 오천 원을 주면 우리가 알아서 할게."

용표는 평소에도 경찰의 월급이 올라야 된다고 생각하는 사람이었다. 어차피 나갈 돈 얼른 계산을 치르고 뜨자 싶어 순순히 응하고 주머니를 뒤지는데 천 원짜리 세 장하고 동전들만 달랑 잡힌다. 전대를 풀어보니 만 원짜리만 고무밴드에 묶여 있다. 만 원짜리 하나를 꺼낸다.

"오천 원짜리가 읎네요."

"알았어."

경찰이 되돌아갔다. 그는 담뱃불을 붙여 물고 경찰을

stared at him. Although he continued to hose out the interior as nonchalantly as possible, he felt his face grow bright red.

He was trying to wash the mess from the ground around the truck when he noticed the young guardsman boarding a bus. He wanted to chase him down and smack him full in the face, but by then the bus had rumbled off.

"Fill'er up, please."

He attempted a smile at the attendant, who had been giving him an unfriendly stare the whole while. *Honestly, could this day get any worse?* His head was spinning, and now his insides were turning—he himself felt like vomiting.

Without a doubt, today was a terrible day, through and through. He just wanted to sleep. After tidying up the cartons in the truck bed once more, he started off in the direction of Daejeon. *Forget about the rest of today's route. I just want to go home, lie down, and get some rest.* He had been trying so hard all day to keep his mouth shut, but on days like this that were total train wrecks, it was best to just avoid doing anything altogether. *Is today the only day? I should just stay home.*

Coming up on a city bus that was making a stop,

기다렸다. 오늘 하루 그래도 원하는 대로 된 것이 이번 흥정이구나 싶다. 비록 순찰차에 걸리기는 했지만 오천 원으로 해결 봤으니 이익이라면 이익이었다. 까짓것, 오천 원 잃어버린 셈치자. 그런 생각을 하다가 갑자기 눈이 휘둥그레졌다. 머뭇머뭇하던 순찰차가 그대로 출발해버린 것이 아닌가. 아 아니. 저 새끼들이.

말도 안 되는 거였다. 아무리 일진이 사납기로 만 원을 오천 원으로 깎느라 얼마나 굽신거렸는데 그렇게 해서 간신히 지킨 생돈을 이제 경찰에게 털리기까지 한단 말인가. 용표는 어안이 벙벙했다. 저것들이 계란장수 돈이라고 우습게 아는구나…… 종일 안 풀려 죽겠는데 이제 돈까지, 정말 끝까지 꼬이는구나.

니기미 씨팔. 자신도 모르게 욕을 내지른 것과 동시에 차를 출발시켰다.

얼마 가지 않아 순찰차를 따라잡을 수 있었다. 추월선을 달리고 있는 순찰차 뒤에 달라붙은 그는 확성기를 틀고 마이크를 들었다.

"빽차는 우측으로, 빽차는 우측으로."

깜짝 놀란 경찰의 얼굴이 유리에 비친다.

"반복한다. 빽차는 우측으로, 빽차는 우측으로."

Yong-pyo moved instinctively into the passing lane. He crested a low hill, and just as the city of Daejeon came into view, a voice from a loudspeaker brought him to attention.

"Egg truck, pull over. Egg truck, pull over."

Looking in his rear-view mirror, he saw a patrol car following him.

What a mess. Yong-pyo sighed.

"Egg truck, pull over. Egg truck, pull over," the patrol car urged again from behind. The long rectangular lights on top of the patrol car whirled as if they were alive.

"Honestly, I just have no luck today."

He stopped the car on the shoulder. The door of the patrol car, which had stopped in front of him, opened, and a broad-shouldered policeman saluted and then approached.

"It's been a long day, eh? Your driver's license, please."

Yong-pyo had years of driving experience under his belt. He knew how to handle a situation like this.

"Please, cut me some slack, just this once. I was in the standard lane, but I had to switch because I was passing a city bus."

낭패라는 판단을 했는지 순찰차는 속력을 내기 시작했다.

어, 도망을 가? 저것들이 내 차를 우습게 알어. 그동안 오단 밟을 일이 없었다만, 좋다 해 보자.

그는 기어를 바꾸고 가속기를 힘껏 밟았다. 오고가는 차들이 많아 순찰차는 멀리 가지 못했다.

"빽차는 우측으로. 내 오천 원 내놔."

마이크 볼륨을 한껏 올리고 악을 썼다. 이윽고 순찰차는 우측 갓길에 섰고 용표도 바짝 붙여 차를 세웠다. 지나가는 차들이 속력을 줄이고 창문을 내려 무슨 일인가 구경을 했다. 좀전의 경찰이 달려왔다.

"지금 뭣하는 거야?"

얼굴이 험상궂게 구겨져 있다.

"오천 원 받기로 했으면 약속대로 해야. 만 원짜리 받고 튀는 법이 워디 있슈."

용표도 지지 않고 대든다. 확성기를 통해 두 사람의 목소리가 울려퍼졌다. 빵빵빵. 순찰차에서 경적이 울렸다. 한동안 그를 노려보던 경찰은 호주머니에서 만 원짜리를 꺼내 던지고는 후다닥 돌아간다.

용표는 멀리 사라지는 순찰차를 바라보았다. 지나가

Yong-pyo flashed a smile that he hoped would leave a good impression, and decided that if he ever met this Lady Luck, he would give her a good beating.

"You committed an illegal lane change. Hand me your license, please."

"Come on, do you really have to ticket someone like me, a man living day-to-day? Please, just this once. How much do you think I make selling eggs? Don't do this, please let me off just this once."

The officer looked this way and that way, indifferent, a little restless. Yong-pyo launched into a possible compromise, mustering as much patience as he could.

"I wasn't even able to make my daily quota today. Really, I'm telling you. In fact, I was just on my way home. I've packed it in for the day. Please, do me a favor, who do you think I am, a criminal?"

The officer, staring impassively at the supplicating, head bobbing up and down occasionally, finally nodded.

"In that case, you could settle with a ten-thousand note."

"I couldn't even make enough for gas today."

"Geez, listen to this guy."

는 차들이 박수를 치고 어떤 이는 엄지손가락을 들어올려주었으나 눈에 들어오지도 않는다. 멀리 시내 너머로 희미한 노을이 깔리고 있다. 그는 만 원짜리를 만지작거렸다. 아직도 가슴이 뛰고 한순간에 일어난 일이라 마치 꿈을 꾼 것 같다. 이 돈이 다시 들어오다니⋯⋯

그는 용순을 떠올렸고 마침 돈의 용도를 생각했다. 이 돈으로 모처럼 삼겹살이라도 넉넉히 사 용순네를 찾아가야겠구나. 어른 셋 아이 하나 먹을 삼겹살에 매제와 마실 소주까지 대충 계산해보니 이천 원 정도가 빠졌다. 좋다, 이것은 아람이 아이스크림 값이다.

『바다가 아름다운 이유』, 솔출판사, 1996

"Well then, just give me a ticket for not maintaining a safe distance."

"For five thousand? No way. Ten thousand."

However, he won over the officer in the end.

"You really are something... but we'll do your way. Just give me five thousand and we're square," the officer conceded.

Yong-pyo was someone who, even on a normal day, thought policemen deserved a raise. *Anyways, let's just count the money and get out of here*, he thought, rummaging through his pockets. However, he only came up with three one-thousand bills and a few coins. He looked through his money pouch, but there were only ten-thousand bills, bound by a rubber band. He took out one of them.

"I don't have any fives."

"Okay."

The officer went back to his patrol car. Yong-pyo lit a cigarette and waited. Even if the day had been terrible, he'd finally bargained something down to what he wanted. Caught by a trooper, he'd salvaged he situation with a five-thousand bill—a gain was a gain. Then again, he had lost five thousand *won*. As he thought this, his eyes suddenly bulged. The patrol car, which had been idling, had taken off! *That bastard!*

Unbelievable. No matter how rough a day he had been having, after all the sucking up he had done to reduce the fine to five thousand *won*, now the officer had taken off with the money he had barely been able to keep. Yong-pyo's eyes glazed over. *They must look down on my money because I'm an egg-peddler...today has been an absolute mess and I just want to lie down, but now my money too...* Was today going to really be terrible down to its very end?

That motherfucker. Yong-pyo started the car as curses slipped out of his mouth.

He had not gone far when he caught up to the patrol car. He came up close to the patrol car, which had been riding in the passing lane, and turned up his loudspeaker. "Patrol car, pull over. Patrol car, pull over."

He saw the shocked face of the officer through the glass.

"I repeat, pull over. Patrol car, pull over."

The patrol car sped up.

Oh-ho, trying to run, are you? No respect for my truck. Well, it's about time I saw what she can do in fifth gear. Let her rip!

He switched gears and floored it. With all the

traffic, the patrol car wasn't going very far.

"Patrol car, pull over. Give me my five thousand *won!*" he blared, turning up the loudspeaker to the maximum. Finally, the patrol car pulled over, Yong-pyo close on his tail. Passing cars slowed down and lowered their windows to gawk... The officer came running over.

"What the hell are you doing?" His face bore a threatening expression.

"We decided on five thousand, and you're going to make good on your word. How could you take off with my ten-thousand like that?" Yong-pyo said, defiant in spite of it all. Their two voices resonated through the loudspeaker. The patrol car honked at the officer, who glared at Yong-pyo before removing a ten-thousand bill from his pocket, tossing it toward him, then running back to his car.

Yong-pyo stared at the patrol car as it disappeared into the distance. Passing drivers applauded him and one man gave him a thumbs-up, but he didn't notice. The hazy sunset was hidden behind the city off in the distance. He fiddled with the ten thousand note. His heart was still pounding, and because everything had happened so quickly, it seemed like it had all been a dream. *The money came back to me after all...*

He recalled Yong-sun, and immediately knew what he was going to do with the money. He would buy a generous amount of *samgyupsal* and go over to Yong-sun's place. He did some rough calculations in his head—enough *samgyupsal* for 3 adults and 1 child, plus the *soju* for his brother-in-law—and he would have two thousand left over. *Perfect. That'd be just enough for A-ram's ice cream.*

Translated by Kerong Lin

해설

Afterword

불운과 행운

강경석 (문학평론가)

한창훈은 대도시의 소비적 일상에 대한 탐구가 한국 문학의 주류를 차지하기 시작한 1990년대에 등장해 거꾸로 농어촌과 소도시 하층민들의 삶에 천착한 희귀한 작가들 중 한 사람이다. 대도시의 삶을 대변하는 '표준어' 대신 충청도와 전라도의 사투리를 충실히 살려내는 그의 소설언어는 일찍부터 "서민적 훈기와 활력"(황종연)을 해학적이면서도 빼어나게 형상화했다는 평가를 받은 바 있다.

「오늘의 운세」는 1996년에 발간된 그의 첫 소설집 『바다가 아름다운 이유』에 수록된 초기 단편이다. 이 작품의 제목은 그와 절친한 문우인 유용주(1960~)의 첫 시

Bad Luck and Good Luck

Kang Kyeong-seok (literary critic)

Han Chang-hoon entered the literary scene in the 1990s at a time when the excessive big-city lifestyle was becoming a hot topic in Korean literature. Han, however, was one of the rare authors who chose instead to delve into the lives of the everyday people from farming and fishing villages and small towns. The language in his stories, which truthfully reproduces the dialects of the Chungcheong and Jeolla-do instead of taking on the "standard dialect," the voice of the big city, not only draws laughs but has been praised from early on as a remarkable embodiment of what Hwang Jong-yeon described as "folksy warmth and vitality."

집 제목에서 따왔다. 제도권 교육을 받지 못한 채 날품팔이 노동자로 온갖 직업을 전전하며 살아온 시인 유용주에 대해 그가 느끼는 우애를 짐작할 수 있는 대목이다.

이 단편의 주인공은 소형트럭에 계란을 싣고 다니며 파는 용표라는 장사꾼이고 배경은 충청북도 옥천군 일대이다. 그런데 이곳은 농촌지역이되 이미 도시적 삶을 깊숙이 호흡하고 있다. 세천공원이라는 위락시설이 들어서면서 이 일대는 유람객들을 위한 상가지역으로 변모하고 있다. 이 소설은 이러한 세태 변화를 도입부에 등장하는 세천상회의 면면을 묘사함으로써 간명하게 제시하고 있다. "공원 입구의 번듯한 음식점들 때문에 한 뼘쯤 내려앉아 보이는 세천상회는 요즘것에 밀려난 고랫것으로 보인다." 세천상회는 "옛적 점방 수준"이라는 표현에서도 알 수 있듯이 농촌의 기억을 여전히 간직하고 있는 장소이다.

그러나 작가의 관심사는 "요즘것에 밀려난 고랫것"에 대한 막연한 향수를 소설화하는 데 머물지 않는다. 세천상회는 지금 뜻밖에 호황이다. 형편이 넉넉지 않은 노인 유람객들에게 세천공원 입구에 새로 생긴 번듯한 식당들은 "그저 구경삼아 쳐다보는 나무나 물과 매한가

"Today's Fortune," published in 1996, is the first in a collection of short stories from *The Reason the Ocean is Beautiful*. The work was named after the first poetry collection of his close friend Yoon Yong-Ju (1960~). It hints at the close bond Han felt towards the poet Yoon, who had never received a formal education and had lived the majority of his life drifting between all kinds of jobs as a day laborer.

The protagonist of Han's short story is a delivery truck egg peddler named Yong-pyo. The story takes place in the Okcheon-gun in the Chungcheongbuk-do, a rural area, but one in which city life has left a deep impression. With the establishment of the recreational area known as Secheon Park, the Okcheon-gun has been changing into a commercial-gun catering to sightseers for a number of years. This kind of social change is aptly portrayed in the description of Secheon Corner at the beginning of the story. "Because of the fairly decent restaurant at the entrance of the park, it seemed like Secheon Corner, looking like it was on the verge of collapse, had been pushed into the shadows by newer things." As you might be able to tell from the depiction of Secheon Corner as an

지"였으므로 "엉덩이 붙일 마땅한 곳 없는 그들에게 더 없이 좋은 곳이 한갓지고 값 헐한 세천상회 마루"였기 때문이다. 작가는 세천상회의 면면을 통해 농촌에서 도시로 이행 중인 어떤 중간지대의 삶을 드러냄으로써 도시적인 것과 농촌적인 것의 긴장과 대립 혹은 그 상호작용을 균형 있는 필치로 탐사한다.

'오늘의 운세'라는 제목은 통상 그날그날의 길흉화복을 점치는 일간지 끄트머리의 코너명이다. 하루하루 먹고 사는 일이 무엇보다도 중요한 서민들에겐 그날의 운수에 대한 궁금증이 끊일 수 없기 때문이다. 이 작품의 주인공 용표의 하루는 그러나 소소한 불운들의 연속이다. 세천공원 입구에서 옥천 시가지 아파트촌으로 이어지는 장삿길도 시원찮았을 뿐만 아니라 전날엔 하나뿐인 여동생 용순이 남편에게 매를 맞고 찾아오기까지 했다. 그런가 하면 술 취한 방위병을 트럭에 태워주었다가 낭패를 보기까지 했으니 그의 '오늘의 운세'는 흉하기 짝이 없는 셈이다.

그런데 소설의 핵심사건은 막바지에 가서야 벌어진다. 아무래도 운수가 꼬인 듯해 집으로 돌아가려고 결심한 용표는 앞길을 가로막는 버스를 불법 추월하다가

"old-fashioned restaurant," the Okcheon-gun, while becoming increasingly modernized, remains a place where the memories of rural life are preserved.

However, this fictional setting of the author's concern does not dwell in the hazy memories of the past, existing merely as a "place that has been shoved aside by modernity." On the contrary, Secheon Corner bustles with industry and business. This is because the older visitors, who are not as well-off as other sightseers, see the new restaurants at the entrance of the park as "no different from the trees or streams that attracted tourists," and as merely a place where they "wanted a nice spot to park their butts, there was no better place than the floor of the quiet and cheap Secheon Corner." Through Secheon Corner and all of its different facets, the author even-handedly explores the tension and friction between city and country life, uncovering the stories of those on the brink of transforming into city-dwellers.

The title of this piece, "Today's Fortune," is the name of the segment in the daily newspaper where you can read your daily fortune. The daily fortune is a source of never-ending curiosity for many

교통경찰에게 딱지를 끊길 처지가 된다. 뇌물 오천 원으로 상황은 마무리되는 듯했지만 만 원짜리를 받은 경찰이 거스름돈 오천 원을 돌려주지 않고 줄행랑을 치고 만다. 여기서 모종의 반전이 일어난다. 용표는 한편 코믹하면서도 한편 서글픈 이 무수한 불운들에 맞서기로 결심한 듯 경찰차를 뒤쫓는다. 계란트럭에 달린 확성기로 "빽차는 우측으로, 빽차는 우측으로" 하고 외치며 달리는 장면은 작품의 절정이다. 망신살이 뻗친 경찰이 차를 세우고 만 원짜리 지폐를 팽개치듯 돌려준 뒤 달아나자 용표는 마치 행운아가 된 것 같은 승리의 기쁨에 들뜬다. 용표의 불운들은 스스로 자초한 것이 아니지만 그의 마지막 행운은 스스로 쟁취한 것이란 점이 중요하다. 이 소설은 일상적 불운을 행운으로 전도시키는 하층민 특유의 자발성과 낙천성을 넓은 시야와 균형감 있는 서술로 유머러스하게 묘파한 작품이라 할 수 있다.

서민들의 무구한 인간적 욕망들로부터 삶과 세계를 새로 열 가능성을 발견하려는 작가의 고투는 지금 이 시간까지도 간단없이 지속되고 있다.

people, often for those who live from hand to mouth day-to-day. However, the hero of this story, Yong-pyo, has a day that is nothing but a relentless string of small misfortunes. Not only has his only sister come looking for him the night prior after another beating by her husband, but also his sales route from the entrance of Secheon Park to the apartments in Okcheon is utterly fruitless. Moreover, he offers a ride to a drunk soldier that eventually leads to even greater trouble. His "daily fortune" seems unbelievably ominous.

The climax of the story does not take place until the end. Yong-pyo decides to return home after his series of unlucky dealings but illegally passes a bus and so is faced with a patrol officer and a ticket. Yong-pyo believes he smoothed things over with a 5,000 *won* bribe, but the police officer, to whom he has given a 10,000 *won* note expecting change, drives off instead. Here, a sort of role reversal takes place. Yong-pyo, who is at once a source of both comedy and sympathy, pursues the officer, perhaps having finally decided to take a stand against his series of unfortunate events. The description of Yong-pyo's chase scene, with Yong-pyo tearing after the patrolmen and blaring "patrol car, pull over, patrol car, pull over" from his loudspeaker, is the climax of the story. The flustered police officer pulls over and tosses the 10,000 *won* note back at Yong-pyo before fleeing, leaving Yong-pyo finally flushed with a feeling of success, as if Lady Luck was smiling down on him at last. Although Yong-pyo never personally brings his unfortunate events down upon himself, the critical event in the story is that his final lucky break comes from something he achieves himself. Ultimately, one might say that Han's "Today's Fortune" light-heartedly describes the color, spontaneity, and optimism of everyday people turning their bad luck into good luck.

The author's struggle to uncover new lives and worlds, starting with the naiveté and human desires of ordinary citizens, continues even now.

비평의 목소리

Critical Acclaim

한창훈의「목련꽃 그늘 아래서」는 이제는 멸종 위기
에 몰린 '농촌을 다룬 문학'이다. 자본의 물결이 도도한
이 시대에 시류에 영합하지 않고 아직도 농촌소설을 만
지는 작가가 있다는 반가움이 앞서지 않는 것은 아니지
만, 작품을 이끌어가는 구성력, 인물을 매만지는 품새
그리고 인정물태의 기미를 섬세하게 살필 줄 아는 수긋
한 문체 등, 이 신인급 작가의 기초가 탄탄한 것이 더욱
미더웠다. 요즘은 이만큼 빠진 단편도 드물다.

최원식

소설이 첨단의 풍속을 반영하기에 급급한 혐의가 적

Han Chang-hoon's *In the Shade of the Magnolias* is "literature that deals with rural life," a genre of literature that has been nearly driven to the brink of extinction. The fact that the author focuses on rural life instead of catering to the trends of this capital-intensive generation brings me much joy, but beyond that, the organization of his story, his characterization, writing style that delicately studies every inch of the man and world he lives in has given me reason to believe that this rookie author's foundation is solid. Short stories that capture my attention to this extent are rare nowadays.

Choi Weon-sik·

지 않은 시대에 한창훈과 같은 신예의 출현으로 우리
마음은 든든하다. 1990년대 소설에서 서민적 삶의 훈기
와 활력을 소생시켰다는 점에서 그의 성과는 뚜렷하다.

황종연

거두절미하고 말해 한창훈의 소설은 참 재미있다. 그
러나 그의 소설 곳곳에서 빛나는 재미는 몸 가벼운 위
트나 얄팍한 재치 따위와는 격이 다르다. 그것은 삶의
뼈저림과 고단함을 온몸으로 부딪쳐 겪어낸 자만이 비
로소 알아챌 수 있는 성숙한 지혜의 다른 이름이다. 나
는 근래의 젊은 작가들 가운데 한창훈만큼 팍팍한 일상
속에서 의뭉스럽게 웃음의 미학을 찾아내는 재능 있는
작가를 보지 못했다.

진정석

그의 소설을 읽을 때마다 나는 바다를 만난다. 아득한
그리움의 바다, 혹은 생의 미친 몸부림인 바다, 그곳에,
혹은 그 안에 무엇이 있을까. 생의 알몸을 부드럽게 더
듬는 물속의 물의 흐름. 그것을 그처럼 섬세하게, 따뜻
하게, 치열하게 뭍으로 길어올리는 작가는 흔치 않을

The emergence of a new writer like Han Chang-hoon in an era preoccupied with modern trends is encouraging. Out of the short stories of the 1990's that revive the warmth and vitality of the common people, his work stands out.

Hwang Jong-yeon

To put it bluntly, Han Chang-hoon's stories are very fun. However, his stories, which are thoroughly delightful, are on a different level from those that just demonstrate a flash of wit or a flimsy bit of comedy. They contain a maturity and wisdom that only those who have faced life's hardships and pains head-on can understand. I cannot find anyone amongst the new writers of today who can capture the subtle aesthetics of comedy in tales of hard-knock lives as well as Han Chang-hoon.

Jin Jeong-seok

Whenever I read his stories, I see the ocean. The ocean that I long for in the distance, or the bizarre twists and turns of life's ocean. There, or within this ocean, what might there be? The flow of the water, softly lapping at your naked body. Authors that can bring you to shore with delicacy, warmth, and pas-

것이다. 세상의 모든 애절함이 그의 바다 앞에서 먹먹
한 가슴을 위로받으리라. 그는 이미 그 깊은 속에 있으
니.

김인숙

한창훈의 소설을 읽는 맛은 냉동식품이나 방부 처리
된 포장식품만 먹다가 싱싱한 자연산 푸성귀를 먹는 맛
과 같다고나 할까. 도시적인 감수성을 여유 있게 비껴
가면서도 재미가 여간 아니다.

박완서

한창훈은 고집스러운 소설가다. 그의 작품세계는 처
음부터 지금까지 한결같다. 다채로운 실험의 와중에도
변하지 않는 개성이 유독 그의 것이라고만은 할 수 없
지만, 그의 작품을 통독해보면 몇 가지의 주요한 모티
프를 한시도 놓지 않고 있음을 쉽게 알 수 있다. 그의 소
설에서 자주 등장하는 방랑하는 젊은이 혹은 소설가의
형상은 작가의 자화상이기도 하지만, 말과 글로 딱 집
어 드러낼 수 없는 삶의 신비와 수수께끼에 대한 작가
의 집념과 맞닿아 있기도 하다. 경박한 유행풍조가 불

sion, as he does, are few and far between. All of the world's sorrows comfort your deafened heart in front of his ocean. He is already deep inside.

Kim In-suk

You might say that reading Han Chang-hoon's stories is like eating fresh, natural vegetables after only eating frozen or preserved foods. Even as he deflects the sensitivities of city life, his humor is of a rare kind.

Park Wan-suh

Han Chang-hoon is a stubborn writer. His works have remained unchanged from the beginning until now. While he's not the only one who has maintained the same style between different experimentations, if you were to read through the entire body of his works, you would easily see that several main motifs are always present. Across his stories, one can see that while the young characters often appear like self-portraits of the author himself, you would also encounter the writer's attachment to the mysteries and riddles of life that cannot be pinpointed through words or speech alone. Considering the literary scene and how triv-

길처럼 일어났다 거품처럼 꺼지곤 하는 문학 세태에 비
추어 이것은 믿음직한 매력임에 틀림없다.

김명환

ial trends rise like fire before popping like bubbles, Han's work certainly bears the charm of reliability.

Kim Myung-hwan

한창훈

작가 한창훈은 1963년 전라남도 여수시 삼산면 거문도에서 태어났다. 일곱 살에 낚시를 시작했고 아홉 살 때는 해녀였던 외할머니에게 잠수를 배웠다. 제대로 된 문학수업은커녕 중고등학교 시절 글짓기 대회에서 상 한 번 받아본 일 없던 그는 고교시절에 광주에서 5·18을 겪었다. 그때 함께 가두행진에 나섰던 또래의 학생이 계엄군의 총에 맞아 쓰러지는 광경을 목격하기도 했다.

음악실 디제이, 트럭운전사, 커피숍 주방장, 홍합공장 노동자, 오징어잡이배나 양식 채취선을 타는 뱃사람 일을 두루 거쳤고 여대 앞에서 브로치를 팔거나 포장마차를 운영하기도 했다.

그가 소설을 써보겠다고 마음먹은 것은 스물여섯이 지나서였다. 섬에서 태어난 그는 '바다'를 자신의 문학적 대주제로 삼았다. 바다는 높낮이가 따로 없는 평등의 상징이었기 때문이다. 1992년《대전일보》신춘문예에 단편「닻」이 당선되어 작가의 길에 들어섰다. 전업작가가 된 한창훈은 한국작가회의에서 일하며 대학에서

Han Chang-hoon

Han Chang-hoon was born in 1963 on Geomun-do, Samsan-myeon, Yeosu-si, Jeolla-do. He began fishing at the age of seven, and at nine, learned how to dive from his maternal grandmother, a female diver. In high school, Han witnessed the May 18th Gwangju Massacre. There, he witnessed his fellow students, with whom he had marched in the streets, being shot down by troops enforcing martial law. Han worked a wide variety of jobs: music DJ, truck driver, café head chef, mussel plant worker, and seaman, Han even sold brooches in front of a woman's university and ran a food stall for a short period of time.

Han's early literary pursuits were minimal to say the least. He never received a single prize at writing competitions during his middle and high school years, never mind even proper literature classes. Han didn't decide to write stories until he was over twenty-six years old. The ocean became the main theme for Han, who had been born on an island. The ocean to Han was clearly a symbol of equality

소설 창작을 가르치기도 했다. 그 사이에도 고향 거문도를 수시로 드나들었다.

현대상선의 컨테이너선을 타고 부산에서 두바이, 홍콩에서 로테르담까지 두 번의 대양 항해에 참여하기도 했으며 특히 인도양과 수에즈운하를 거쳐 지중해와 북대서양에 이르렀던 두 번째 항해에 큰 인상을 받았다. 지금은 고향 거문도로 돌아와 글을 쓰거나 낚시를 하며 이웃들과 어울려 살고 있다.

단편소설집으로는 『바다가 아름다운 이유』(1996), 『가던 새 본다』(1998), 『세상의 끝으로 간 사람』(2001), 『청춘가를 불러요』(2005), 『나는 여기가 좋다』(2009), 『그 남자의 연애사』(2013), 장편소설로는 『홍합』(1998), 『열여섯의 섬』(2003), 『섬, 나는 세상 끝을 산다』(2003), 『꽃의 나라』(2011) 등이 있다. 『한창훈의 향연』(2009), 『인생이 허기질 때 바다로 가라』(2010) 등의 산문집이 있으며 『검은 섬의 전설』(2005), 『제주선비 구사일생 표류기』(2008)와 같은 어린이 책을 쓰기도 했다. 대산창작기금(1997), 한겨레문학상(1998), 제비꽃서민소설상(2007), 허균문학작가상(2009), 요산문학상(2009)을 수상했다.

without any highs or lows. In the year of 1992, he began his path as a writer when his short story "The Anchor" was chosen in the *Daejeon Ilbo*'s Annual Spring Literary Contest.

Having become a full-time writer, Han Changhoon worked at the Association of Korean Writers and also taught story-writing at a university. In the meantime, he often went back to his hometown on Geomundo. He went on two ocean voyages, one from Busan to Dubai and one from Hong Kong to Rotterdam on one of Hyundai Merchant Marine Co.'s container ships. The second trip, during which he passed through the Indian Ocean and Suez Canal and reached the Mediterranean Sea and the North Atlantic, left a particularly deep impression on him. He has since returned to Geomundo where he passes his days writing, fishing, or socializing with his neighbors.

His short story anthologies include *The Reason the Ocean is Beautiful* (1996), *Looking At a Passing Bird* (1998), *The One Who Went to the End of the World* (2001), *Sing the Song of Your Youth* (2005), *I Like It Here* (2009), and *His Love Life* (2013). His novels include *Mussels* (1998), *The Island of the 16-Year-Olds* (2003), *Island, I Live the End of the World* (2003), *The Country of Flowers* (2011), and more. His collections of prose works include *Han Chang-hoon's Feast* (2009), *When Your Life is Starved, Go to the Ocean* (2010), and he has also written children's books such as *The Legend of the Dark Island* (2005) and *The Adventures of the Jeju Scholar's Narrow Escape* (2008).

He has been awarded the Daesan Creative Writing Fund (1997), the *Hangyeore* Literary Award (1998), the Violet Common People's Award (2007), the Heo Gyun Literary Writers' Award (2009), and the Yosan Literature Award (2009).

번역 **케롱 린** Translated by Kerong Lin

케롱 린은 2013년 캐나다 밴쿠버의 브리티시컬럼비아 대학교에서 영어학과 아시아 언어와 문화(한국어 전공)로 학사 학위를 수여했다. UBC에서 브루스 풀턴 교수로부터 한국문학 번역 강의를 수강하면서 한국문학과 번역에 깊은 관심을 갖게 되었다. TaLK 프로그램을 통해 충청북도 진천의 초등학교에서 영어교사로 재직 중이며 이 프로그램을 마친 뒤 밴쿠버로 돌아가 학업을 계속해 교사자격증을 획득할 예정이다.

Kerong Lin is a recent graduate of the University of British Columbia in Vancouver, Canada, where she earned a B.A. ('13) with a double major in English Language and Asian Language & Culture (specializing in Korean). At UBC, she took classes in Korean Literary Translation under Bruce Fulton, in which she discovered her interest in Korean literature and translation. She is currently working as a part-time English teacher at an elementary school in Jincheon, Chungcheongbuk-do under the TaLK (Teach and Learn in Korea) Program, but will soon return to Vancouver to continue her studies and to pursue a teaching certificate.

감수 **전승희, 데이비드 윌리엄 홍**

Translated by Jeon Seung-hee and David William Hong

전승희는 서울대학교와 하버드대학교에서 영문학과 비교문학으로 박사 학위를 받았으며, 현재 하버드대학교 한국학 연구소의 연구원으로 재직하며 아시아 문예 계간지 《ASIA》 편집위원으로 활동 중이다. 현대 한국문학 및 세계문학을 다룬 논문을 다수 발표했으며, 바흐친의 『장편소설과 민중언어』, 제인 오스틴의 『오만과 편견』 등을 공역했다. 1988년 한국여성연구소의 창립과 《여성과 사회》의 창간에 참여했고, 2002년부터 보스턴 지역 피학대 여성을 위한 단체인 '트랜지션하우스' 운영에 참여해 왔다. 2006년 하버드대학교 한국학 연구소에서 '한국 현대사와 기억'을 주제로 한 워크숍을 주관했다.

Jeon Seung-hee is a member of the Editorial Board of *ASIA*, and a Fellow at the Korea Institute, Harvard University. She received a Ph.D. in English Literature from Seoul National University and a Ph.D. in Comparative Literature from Harvard University. She has presented and published numerous papers on modern Korean and world literature. She is also a co-translator of Mikhail Bakhtin's *Novel and the People's Culture* and Jane Austen's *Pride and Prejudice*. She is a founding member of the Korean Women's Studies Institute and of the biannual Women's Studies' journal *Women and Society* (1988), and she has been working at 'Transition House,' the first and oldest shelter for battered women in New England. She organized a workshop entitled "The Politics of Memory in Modern Korea" at the Korea Institute, Harvard University, in 2006. She also served as an advising committee member for the Asia-Africa Literature Festival in 2007 and for the POSCO Asian Literature Forum in 2008.

데이비드 윌리엄 홍은 미국 일리노이주 시카고에서 태어났다. 일리노이대학교에서 영문학을, 뉴욕대학교에서 영어교육을 공부했다. 지난 2년간 서울에 거주하면서 처음으로 한국인과 아시아계 미국인 문학에 깊이 몰두할 기회를 가졌다. 현재 뉴욕에서 거주하며 강의와 저술 활동을 한다.

David William Hong was born in 1986 in Chicago, Illinois. He studied English Literature at the University of Illinois and English Education at New York University. For the past two years, he lived in Seoul, South Korea, where he was able to immerse himself in Korean and Asian-American literature for the first time. Currently, he lives in New York City, teaching and writing.

바이링궐 에디션 한국 대표 소설 056
오늘의 운세

2014년 3월 7일 초판 1쇄 인쇄 | 2014년 3월 14일 초판 1쇄 발행

지은이 한창훈 | 옮긴이 케롱 린 | 펴낸이 김재범
감수 전승희, 데이비드 윌리엄 홍 | 기획 정은경, 전성태, 이경재
편집 정수인, 이은혜 | 관리 박신영 | 디자인 이춘희
펴낸곳 (주)아시아 | 출판등록 2006년 1월 27일 제406-2006-000004호
주소 서울특별시 동작구 서달로 161-1(흑석동 100-16)
전화 02.821.5055 | 팩스 02.821.5057 | 홈페이지 www.bookasia.org
ISBN 979-11-5662-002-0 (set) | 979-11-5662-013-6 (04810)
값은 뒤표지에 있습니다.

Bi-lingual Edition Modern Korean Literature 056
Today's Fortune

Written by Han Chang-hoon | Translated by Kerong Lin
Published by Asia Publishers | 161-1, Seodal-ro, Dongjak-gu, Seoul, Korea
Homepage Address www.bookasia.org | Tel. (822).821.5055 | Fax. (822).821.5057
First published in Korea by Asia Publishers 2014
ISBN 979-11-5662-002-0 (set) | 979-11-5662-013-6 (04810)